Hi girls!
Today we went to
visit a sloth habitat!
Sorry, but we're not
bringing one home.
We miss you
so much! Love,
Mom and Eric

Goldblatt Girls
28 Goodwin Road
Henson, PA 18229
USA

I can't believe they're not
bringing us home a sloth.
What is the point of a honeymoon
if there are no sloth souvenirs?

Take me home!
I will love you
forever and eat
leaves all day.

3 Great Things about Living with the Graham-Changs

We've had waffles for breakfast three times since we've been here. It's awesome.

Q.) Melody seems really happy for the first time in ages. She's finally cool with Mom's new husband, Coach Eric. I don't think she'll try to run away again, and she even seems okay with still being grounded while they're away on their honeymoon.

Does sumbuddy need a hug?

No thanks, I...

HUG ATTACK!

A few months ago she would NEVER have put up with that.

3.) Now that we've been here for a week I think that Bad Cat is starting to get used to us, and maybe even accept us.

Good kitty, nice kitty.

Don't. Make. Direct. Eye contact.

Then again, it might take a little while longer.

Mom and Coach Eric are going to be away on their honeymoon for one more week, not getting us a sloth.

Unacceptable.

But things have calmed down a lot since the drama that happened around their wedding.

THE MOST DRAMATIC THING THAT CAN HAPPEN NOW

1. No more waffles!
2. My pencil broke!
3. Bad Cat attack!

Do you think that we're maybe tempting fate?

Nah.

And then...

Adams Middle School is the other junior high in our town.

They're not really in our town. They're in the next town over.

Does this mean they don't have to go to school?

So. LUCKY.

They'll probably have to find somewhere else to finish up the school year.

The next town over is not that far away.

Papa Dad and Daddy have been talking about what might happen to the Adams kids, but they don't want to talk about it in front of us.

They are not good at keeping things from us.

Going back to school after winter holidays is always a little weird, but it's even weirder this time.

First Weird Thing: Mrs. Goldblatt is now Mrs. Wexler.

Did you hear about the assembly?

Ms. Harrington told us about it last period.

What do you think it's all about?

Jen thinks that it's definitely not about making the cafeteria vegan.

Why would she think that?

She doesn't think that.

Jen is the confusingest.

It's probably also not about starting a vegetable garden in the middle of that big oval.

Do you mean the track?

DRAMATIC ANNOUNCEMENT
So by now you're all aware of the terrible fire that has destroyed Adams Middle School. With only five months left of the school year, the students and teachers at Adams need facilities to complete their studies. They have requested that we, the good-hearted and generous Hamlin Junior High family, take them in.

At first, everyone was kind of shocked.

Then everyone got really curious.

What do we know about these Adams kids?

Aren't they supposed to be rich or something?

And what exactly happened to their school, anyway?

Everyone seems to have a strong opinion about what's going on, but no one has any real idea of what's actually going to happen.

Adams has some really good field hockey players. Our team could be unstoppable.

Are they going to be on our team? And if they're on our team, how can we possibly keep all of our Hamlin players? We'll have to cut people.

That's so unfair!

People are becoming unhinged.

The girls at Adams are really pretty.

Prettier than us?

Yes? No. I don't know!

But they'll be newer, and new is exciting, and therefore prettier, and no one will care about us anymore.

I. Don't. Like. This.

Even our parents are worried.
How are they going to fit all those kids?
They're bringing trailers to put on the soccer field.
How are they going to play soccer?
I don't know. Since when do we care about soccer?
Since our daughter is about to lose her potential future soccer scholarship!
Uh, I don't play soccer.
Well, you certainly don't now.

My mom is coming home tonight. We've emailed her about what happened to Adams Middle School and how half of the students are coming to stay with us, but she hasn't responded, so we're not sure if she got the message.

Maybe we should write it on our welcome home banner.

WELCOME HOME! ADAMS MIDDLE SCHOOL BURNT DOWN AND NOW HALF OF THEIR STUDENTS ARE GOING TO HAMLIN WITH US.

That seems sort of wordy.

Mom and Coach Eric are home!
Stuff they brought for us from Suriname

No sloths. No sloths.

My mom and Coach Eric were not happy about the changes happening at school.

"How can they do this? How many students are going to be in each class?"

THEY'RE GETTING RID OF THE SOCCER FIELD???

I don't know who was more upset.

The one person who doesn't seem at all worried about the changes is Roland.

I won't be the new, different kid anymore!

You haven't been the new kid for years!

But I'm still different.

Not to me.

You don't count, you're my girlfriend.

What are you doing after
school?

Homework, I guess. Why?

Ms. Harrington wants me to
make a bunch of signs and
banners to welcome the Adams kids.

And you want me to help
because of my superior
artistic talents?

Well, I was hoping to keep
the paintbrushes clean.

Because of my superior
paintbrush-cleaning talents?

Exactly.

Can we write "Welcome to Our School Which Is Now Your School Temporarily!"
That seems kind of wordy.
Or "Welcome, New Students Who Are Not New at Being Students!"
Yeesh.

The signs are looking good, and we've started putting them up around the school.

Did you make some new signs?
Nope. Why?
FIRE IT UP, HAMLI
GO BULLDOGS!
Hamlin Junior HIGH
ALL THE W
Fire it up?
Roland would not have written that.

For every one of our "Welcome Adams Students" signs, there were at least two pro-Hamlin signs.

I've never seen so many bulldogs.

Did you even know that our school mascot was a bulldog?

I definitely know it now.

Bulldogs don't seem like very welcoming animals.

So we found out who put up the other posters.

Ms. Harrington is not happy about the new posters, but they do show school spirit, so Principal Rao likes them

Yes! Let's welcome the new students with our friendly puppy.

Our friendly puppy has pretty sharp teeth.

He's... smiley!

NEW INFORMATION:

We are going to have to share lockers with Adams kids.

I can't believe I have to share my locker with some girl named Bertha.

My new lockermate's name is Marisol.

It's so lame that they won't just let us pick our own lockermates. You and I could have shared one and we wouldn't have to deal with stupid Bertha and stupid Marisol.

Yeah, that's too bad.

Lydia's locker

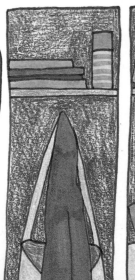

Julie's locker

I'm not that bad.

Sure you're not.

Every time we've halfway adjusted to a new change, along comes another new change.

About half of our classes have been moved to different classrooms. People are not happy.

It's going to take me five minutes to get from Gym to Science.

My English class is about a MILE from my music class.

I am going to have to WALK THROUGH A LAKE OF MOLTEN LAVA AND CLIMB A SHEER ROCK FACE TO GET TO THE CAFETERIA.

In addition to all the other changes, the biggest change seems to be that no one can talk about anything else.

First there were rumors, then there were changes, and now there is

THE WEIRDNESS.

THE WEIRDNESS has nothing to do with the Adams kids coming next week.

It's **THE WEIRDNESS** that dare not speak its name.

Oh, it has a name.

He just did it again.

Again? Where does he want to go this time?

He wants to go on a picnic.

That's nice. ?

A picnic on the moon, so we can watch the Earthrise.

THE WEIRDNESS is named Jamie Burke.

Jamie Burke is pretty much the weirdest kid ever. He told me he liked me at Mom's wedding, and now he keeps asking me out on impossible dates.

Want to go to the White House for dinner?

We should go to Ulan Bator together.

Let's meet up on Tuesday to build a time machine!

We can ride dinosaurs!

Clearly he isn't serious, but...he keeps asking

It's so frustrating because I have no idea what he's thinking. But no one ever has any idea what Jamie is thinking.

But now I have these weird feelings about not knowing what he's thinking.

goldstandard3000: Maybe I just need to confront him, you know? I could just have an honest and open conversation with him about what I want.

jladybugaboo: What do you want?

goldstandard3000: I want to not be confused all the time. Should I just tell him to leave me alone?

jladybugaboo: Is that what you want?

goldstandard3000: No. Yes. Maybe? Stop asking me that! I just want to stop feeling like I'm being messed with.

jladybugaboo: It's weird, because Jamie isn't really the sort of guy who would purposefully mess with people.

goldstandard3000: That's the worst part! He probably doesn't even know he's being so confusing, because he thinks that everyone is as weird as he is!

I make sense to me, therefore I make sense!

Tomorrow is the Big Day.

The first day of the

ADAMS INVASION.

And we are READY.

On second thought, dressing in full Viking battalion gear might make us look completely deranged.

And we are LESS THAN READY.

It feels like the school couldn't possibly fit any more people. All of the hallways are full, all of the classrooms are full, part of the cafeteria is being used as a classroom, part of the gym is being used as a classroom, there are lines to get through the front door.
There are lines **EVERYWHERE.**

In retrospect, that second cup of tea was a terrible idea.

So how did it go with Bertha?

Not so great.

Hi, I'm Lydia. You must be Bertha.

My name is Chelsea.

Oh. Sorry. You look just like my friend Sukie!

So all Asians look alike to you?

Umm...

What was I supposed to say to that? Sukie is really pretty, I thought I was giving her a compliment. She is not like Sukie at all.

I haven't met my lockermate yet,
ut she's already put all of her stuff
n my locker.

At first, no one talked.
I'm sure some of you have questions.
And then everyone talked.
Why can't we share lockers with our friends?
What's going to happen to our sports teams?
Will we be penalized for being late to class if we can't find it?
Or if we can't make it through the crowd?
Are all Hamlin kids stupid or just the ones I've talked to?

Are all the Adams kids so snotty?
Do all the Hamlin kids smell terrible?
Are we still having a school dance?
Will we have to dance with smelly Hamlin kids?

Needless to say, the assembly did not go well.

Settle down, settle down, one question at a time, and could we please try to use KIND WORDS and REMAIN CIVIL? Because if you can't there will be CONSEQUENCES.

After that assembly I can't imagine there being worse consequences than being forced to go to school with Adams kids in the first place.

When the assembly was let out, all the teachers and aides quickly herded us off to our classrooms. They seemed to be trying to keep the Hamlin and the Adams kids as separate as possible.

Can you blame them?

ADAMS INVASION: Day 2

I met Marisol.

Did she smell as bad
as she made your
locker smell?

We did not get that close.

Did you hear about the
one-way hallway?

The what?

There are notices _everywhere_.

ATTENTION ALL STUDENTS

**THE HALLWAY BETWEEN THE MAIN
ENTRANCE AND THE GYM WILL NOW BE A
ONE-WAY HALLWAY IN ORDER TO
PREVENT CONGESTION. PLEASE ABIDE BY
THE ONE-WAY HALLWAY RULE. FAILURE
TO COMPLY WILL RESULT IN DEMERITS.**

Demerits? Oooooh, scary!

DEMERIT SLIP

Student's Name: Lydia Goldblatt

Date(s) 2·2   Time 9   Room ____

No. of Demerits: 1

Reason for Demerits Walking wrong way down one-way hallway

Mrs. Sussaman
(Signature)

Well, that didn't take very long.
My locker is RIGHT THERE.
Why do I have to walk around the
entire gym just to get to my
own locker?
Want to share my locker?
Your locker smells like mermaid poop.
Eww.

jladybugaboo: What did your mom say about the demerit?

goldstandard3000: I may have neglected to tell her about it.

jladybugaboo: Isn't she going to find out anyway?

goldstandard3000: Only if I get three demerits, and then I have to get her signature, which means that I can go the wrong way down the one-way hallway one more time before I get in trouble.

jladybugaboo: Oooooor you could just not go the wrong way down the one-way hallway at all.

goldstandard3000: Nah, I'm just going to save that for an emergency.

jladybugaboo: I was being sarcastic. [INSERT EYE ROLL HERE] That seems like a really good plan.

goldstandard3000: I thought so.

Lydia isn't the only one who got a demerit yesterday.

I got a demerit for running in the hall.

I got a demerit for chewing gum.

I got a demerit for filling my locker with balloons.

Do you remember anyone ever getting a demerit before the Adams kids got here?

I didn't even know demerits existed before the Adams kids got here.

WAYS TO EARN A DEMERIT

1 Going the wrong way down the one-way hallway *Obviously*

2 Chewing gum

3 Running

4 Yelling

5 Having any sort of fun

6 Inappropriate attire

7 Not having a hall pass

8 Vandalism

9 Fighting

In addition to the new students and teachers, the Adams Invasion includes half of the Adams hall monitors.

They are very different from our hall monitors.

| HAMLIN HALL MONITOR | ADAMS HALL MONITOR |

It's official! The first fight between an Adams kid and a Hamlin kid. No one knows who started the fight or who was even in the fight, but EVERYONE is talking about it.

I know who got into the fight in the boys locker room!!!

who?

Don't freak out.

I wasn't freaking out, but now I am. WHO?

Seriously, though, don't start screaming or anything.

WHO???

Roland!!!

This is ridiculous. Everyone is talking about how Roland got into a fight with an Adams kid, but it can't be true. Roland couldn't hurt a fly.

Hallo fly! Please remove yourself from my sandwich.

Oh, I'm so sorry! I didn't realize that was your sandwich.

Not a problem.

You are too kind.

Let's be friends!

But it was definitely him. Jane said that Chuck saw the whole thing

Okay, so it was right before gym, and all the boys were in the locker room, and Chuck said that this blond kid came up to Roland and said something that no one else could understand. Then Roland said something that no one else could understand, and then the blond kid shoved Roland, and Roland shoved him back, and then there were punches and kicks and Chuck's pretty sure that Roland might have lost some teeth.

Oh my god oh my god.
You can't believe everything Jane says. She wasn't even there!
OH MY GOD OH MY GOD OH MY GOD.

jladybugaboo: Just talked to Roland's mom on the phone.

goldstandard3000: Is he okay?

jladybugaboo: I think so, but he's suspended from school for the next two days and his parents won't let him email or talk on the phone.

goldstandard3000: Does he have all his teeth?

jladybugaboo: Mrs. Asbjornsen says that he's fine, just in trouble.

The next day at school was WEIRD.

Hey, you let Roland know we're behind him 100%.

What he did was AWESOME.

You are so lucky to have such an awesome boyfriend.

Roland is seriously so hot.

Um... okay.

Did you even know those kids?

No! I think they're 8th graders.

You're like a celebrity now.

Everyone seems to want to talk to me about Roland.
How's your dude?
Roland is so brave. You tell him I said that.
You were really smart to get in on the ground floor with that one. I wish Chuck had been man enough to fight.
Uh, thanks.
Stay Strong.

Some sixth graders just asked me if I knew Roland!

That has been happening to me ALL DAY.

Everyone is talking about how cool he is.

They don't even know what the fight was about!

Do you know what the fight was about?

I don't even know who he was fighting! Or that he could fight.

Maybe Norwegians are just born warriors and we never knew it because Roland had never before been called to battle.

STOP. Too much weird.

BATTLE ROLAND

Gym is one of the few classes that we have to share with the Adams kids. Roland was getting ready when he was approached by a kid named Stefan.
Hey, are you the Swedish kid?
Ah, Ich dachte das du sah so dumm.
No, I am from Norway, but I see how you could get that mixed up.
goldstandard3000: What does that mean? Is it Norwegian?

jladybugaboo: Stefan wasn't speaking in Norwegian, he was speaking in German.
goldstandard3000: Is he German?
jladybugaboo: No, actually he's from Switzerland but he can speak German.
goldstandard3000: Color me confused.
Excuse me?
Oh, you did not understand what I said? Du sind einfach nur eine blöde Norwegisch.
goldstandard3000: Okay, seriously, what was he saying?
jladybugaboo: He was calling Roland stupid.

goldstandard3000: Wait, how did Roland know what Stefan was saying?

jladybugaboo: Roland can understand German.

goldstandard3000: Who knew?

jladybugaboo: I did not.

goldstandard3000: What other languages does Roland know? Does he know Japanese? That would be cool.

jladybugaboo: Do you want to hear the end of this story?

goldstandard3000: Yes! Please continue.

I want you to know that I understand you and I think that you are rude.

Oh, I didn't know Norwegians could think. How exciting for you!

Please shut up.

jladybugaboo: So at this point everyone else in the locker room has gathered around them.

Why don't you make me.

goldstandard3000: Did Roland make him shut up?

jladybugaboo: Roland shoved him up against a locker!

goldstandard3000: Really???

jladybugaboo: And then Stefan punched Roland.

goldstandard3000: In the face?

jladybugaboo: Not exactly. He kind of punched Roland on the ear.

goldstandard3000: That sounds painful and also weird.

Roland told me that he and Stefan were separated and marched down to Principal Rao's office before any real damage could be done.

I am very disappointed in both of you. Mr. Asbjørnsen, you have not represented Hamlin well, and Mr. von Dusen, as a guest here you are not making a good first impression. You will both be suspended from school for two days and it will go into your permanent record.

Roland is not looking forward to seeing Stefan tomorrow.

I tried to warn Roland about his newfound celebrity but he was still really surprised when he came back to school.

They're escorting us to all of our classes so that no one can mess with Roland. *It's so dramatic.*

Now that Roland has a posse, Stefan also has a posse, and when the two posses pass each other there is some SERIOUS GLOWERING.

That's a lot of glowering.
It was a real glower-off.
Glowertastic! Okay, we're done.

Even though everything is weird and different at school, some things are still the same.

Guess what?

What?

Chicken butt.

You're passing me a note in the middle of Math just to tell me "Chicken butt"?

Well, it's more interesting than my actual news. Chuck and Jane broke up.

Yawn. Must be Tuesday.

Jane and Chuck broke up again?

Seriously?

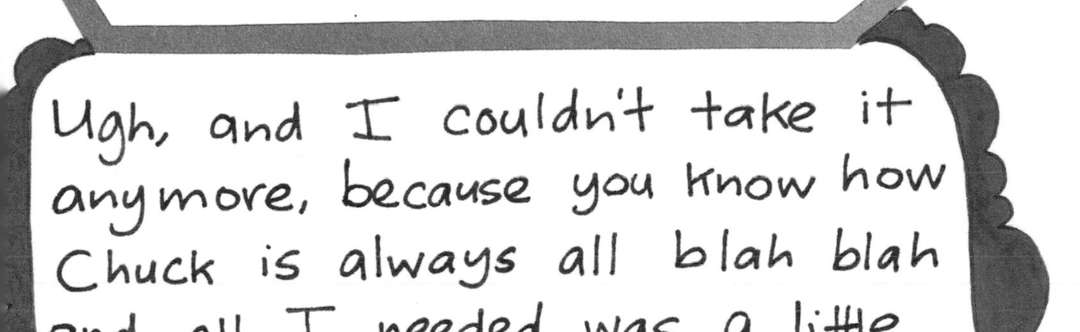

Just talked with Jane.

And here we go. How bad was she?

Hey Jules, did you do the homework?

Yes... How are you?

I'm fine, but I think I messed up the second part of the assignment. Can you take a look?

It was SO WEIRD.
No mention of Chuck?
Nothing.

So you think they're maybe broken up for good now?

I don't know. I guess that depends on why they broke up.

POSSIBLE REASONS FOR JANE AND CHUCK'S BREAKUP

1) Chuck forgot something

> But today is the 3-week anniversary of you giving me this bracelet!

2) Jane forgot something

> All I asked was for you to show up to just one of my Eskrima demos.

3) Their dating was always a terrible idea to begin with?

I think I know why Jane and Chuck broke up.

Roland and I saw them after school. Do you think they're dating? Oh, don't ask me about dating. I know nuthin'.

The news of Jane's ... boyfriend? friend who is a boy? boy something? is out.

I saw them talking outside the gym.

She says there's nothing going on, but I don't believe her.

This is a betrayal.

Roland is actually mad at Jane.
It's so weird to see Roland mad.
His face gets all red.

ANGRY ROLAND

furrowed brow

red skin

un-Roland like scowl

Maybe it's a sign of his impending Vikening.

His what now?

Vikening. When a young Scandinavian becomes a fierce Viking warrior

Are you making this up?

Probably. Yes.

It seems like everyone from Hamlin is against everyone from Adams, and vice versa. No one is liking this whole Jane/Adams Guy thing. The Adams kids probably call it the whole Adam/Hamlin Girl thing. ~~His~~ name is Adam and he's from Adams? Marisol told me.

That girl with Adam is looking for trouble.

Why?

Anyone from Hamlin dating someone from Adams is looking for trouble, duh.

Marisol is kind of rude and our locker still smells really funky, but I think we're sort of getting along.

Where are you from, anyway?

Uh, here.

Come on. You're as Latina as me.

I was born in Bolivia but I'm adopted.

My family is from Ecuador. Your Spanish accent is terrible.

I think we're almost at the point where I can maybe bring up The Stank.

goldstandard3000: So did you talk to Marisol about the smell?

jladybugaboo: Didn't get a chance. I was about to.

goldstandard3000: But then you were overwhelmed by the stank and passed out?

jladybugaboo: No. Worse.

Ugh, Marisol, figures you would want to be friends with her.

And I thought she was a loser when she was at Adams!

jladybugaboo: She didn't want to talk to me anymore after that.

goldstandard3000: Maybe if we both try to be nice to her she'll warm up and you can find out what's making that smell.

I think your lockermate might be worse than mine.

Yeah. Stank can be washed out, but mean is harder to get rid of.

Roland is mad at me.

Are you sure he's mad at you? He might just be generally mad.

No, he's definitely mad at me.

Hei Roland!

I am mad at you.

Why?

He heard that I was trying to be friendly with Marisol and it made him mad.

But Marisol doesn't even like you.

That's probably beside the point.

goldstandard3000: Did you and Roland make nice after school?

jladybugaboo: No. Now I'm mad at him.

goldstandard3000: What did he do?

jladybugaboo: He's trying to tell me who I can and can't be friends with!

goldstandard3000: But you don't even like Marisol.

jladybugaboo: That's not the point!

goldstandard3000: Are you turning into Jane and Chuck? Because if I have to spend the next bunch of months listening to you guys argue about stupid things, let me know now so I can invest in a good pair of earplugs.

jladybugaboo: What if he told me that I couldn't be friends with you?

goldstandard3000: Roland would never do that.

jladybugaboo: Who knows what Angry Roland would do? I'm not talking to him until he removes his angry head from his angry butt.

goldstandard3000: Remind me never to get in a fight with you.

jladybugaboo: I will!

FIGHT WITH ROLAND
Day 2

Seeing how I've got no problems with Roland, he can talk to me

Is Julie still mad at me? She seems like she's mad at me. I really wasn't trying to tell her who she can't be friends with, I was just trying to look out for her, and I don't like it when she's mad at me. Could you maybe talk to her for me please???

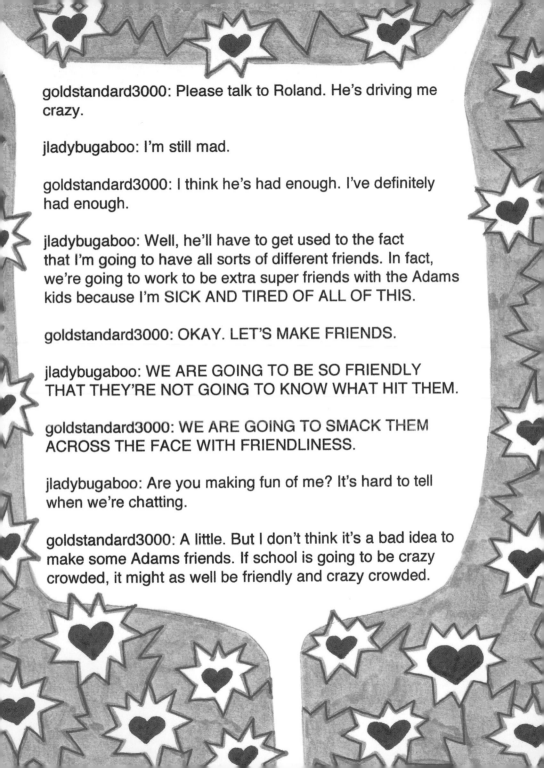

goldstandard3000: Please talk to Roland. He's driving me crazy.

jladybugaboo: I'm still mad.

goldstandard3000: I think he's had enough. I've definitely had enough.

jladybugaboo: Well, he'll have to get used to the fact that I'm going to have all sorts of different friends. In fact, we're going to work to be extra super friends with the Adams kids because I'm SICK AND TIRED OF ALL OF THIS.

goldstandard3000: OKAY. LET'S MAKE FRIENDS.

jladybugaboo: WE ARE GOING TO BE SO FRIENDLY THAT THEY'RE NOT GOING TO KNOW WHAT HIT THEM.

goldstandard3000: WE ARE GOING TO SMACK THEM ACROSS THE FACE WITH FRIENDLINESS.

jladybugaboo: Are you making fun of me? It's hard to tell when we're chatting.

goldstandard3000: A little. But I don't think it's a bad idea to make some Adams friends. If school is going to be crazy crowded, it might as well be friendly and crazy crowded.

Ways to Make Friends with the ADAMS KIDS

We should start a football (Soccer) league! Everyone loves football. (Soccer)

Tree-crocheting Club.

Just get everyone together in a room and get them all talking.

I think Melody was on to something. We need to get everyone together in a room.

We'd need a really big room.

Like the gymnasium.

You're thinking. Scary.

Do you know what happens in the gymnasium?

Really bad games of handball?

School dances.

idea face

worried face

95

The Spring Dance is in two months. Usually half the school is really excited about the Spring Dance.

I just know Mike will ask me.

Are you going to wear your Pink dress?

Because we Can. Not. Clash

And the other half of the school is just annoyed by it.

Gretchen's going to make me wear a tie.

Dance music makes me wanna hurl.

But usually most of the 7th and 8th graders go.

jladybugaboo: Here's what I don't understand. We were going to have the dance anyway—how is it going to make the Hamlin kids and the Adams kids get along? We're probably just going to hang out in separate corners, glaring at each other.

goldstandard3000: I've been thinking about that. We need to do something that will guarantee that kids from both schools interact with each other.

jladybugaboo: Like what?

goldstandard3000: Like if Hamlin and Adams kids went together.

jladybugaboo: What, like a date?

goldstandard3000: Exactly like a date.

THE PLAN

I, Lydia Goldblatt, will ask a boy from Adams to go to the dance with me.

THE PROBLEM

Even talking with kids from Adams will make kids from Hamlin mad at you.

But somebody has to be the first one to do it.

JANE was the first one to do it, and look how everyone is treating her.

I think we've underestimated Jane. She's just being oppressed for being a visionary of peace.

PROBLEM. What about
Jamie Burke?

He hasn't asked me,
so I can ask whomever
I please.

So who is it going to be?
I have no idea. I may
have to ask the expert.

Oh no.

Oh yes.

Can I ask you something?

I'm so glad that you came to me! I have gotten to know some of the Adams guys and they're total sweeties. They don't even care about the whole Chuck thing. This is going to be so much fun!
What is the Chuck thing?

THE CHUCK THING
Everyone knows I dated Chuck, and he's probably told all his friends that I'm an awful girlfriend.
Chuck doesn't seem like the sort of guy who would say mean stuff even if you guys did break up.
Oh Lydia, Lydia, Lydia.
Jane, Jane, Jane.
Everyone says bad stuff about their exes. It's just what's done. Now, let's find you a date!

THE BOYS from ADAMS

JANE'S PICKS

Adam Kelly

So cute, and he's really artistic because he likes black-and-white movies.

Carl Wertheimer

Super super cute and knows a lot about hockey.

Ethan Rubin

You should go for him because I don't like him as much as I like Adam and Carl and also I think you'd make a cute couple.

OBSERVATIONS
of ETHAN RUBIN

1.) Ethan is taller than Lydia. This means that he can reach things I can't. Very helpful.

2.) Ethan eats lunch at the same time as us. This means that he eats. So he's not some sort of cyborg. Exactly.

3.) Ethan has never been observed being mean to a Hamlin kid.

By us, anyway.

Uh, hi?

Pay us no mind.

jladybugaboo: Are you seriously going to ask Ethan out?

goldstandard3000: I think I seriously am.

jladybugaboo: How are you going to do it?

goldstandard3000: What do you mean?

jladybugaboo: I mean, do you have a plan? Are you just going to walk up to him and say, "Hey, strange guy I've never talked to before, want to go to the Spring Dance with a girl from a different school who your classmates see as your mortal enemy?"

goldstandard3000: Well, now you're making me nervous!

jladybugaboo: Sorry.

goldstandard3000: Okay, okay, I have to figure this out.

jladybugaboo: How?

goldstandard3000: I think I have to go back to the expert.

jladybugaboo: Eep.

The Art of Flirtation

(according to Jane)

If you want a guy to be into you, you have to be both accessible and mysterious. You also have to be self-confident and shy, and it's good if you don't look too smart but also not all Duuuuuhhh stupid. And you should make sure they know that you're into the same sort of stuff that they're into, but you can't tell them that.

The words that are coming out of your mouth are making no sense ouch brain.

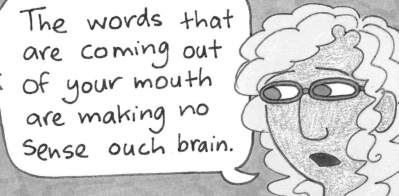

FLIRTATION PRACTICE

FRIENDLY

SHY

MYSTERIOUS

LISTENING

SMART

NOT TOO SMART

Duh.

CUTE

GIGGLING

Tee hee!

LAUGHING

BLAH
HAH.

SERIOUS

DREAMY

INTENSE

goldstandard3000: I think I'm ready.

jladybugaboo: Really?

goldstandard3000: Really.

jladybugaboo: But really?

goldstandard3000: Really really. I'm really going to do it.

jladybugaboo: Ethan.

goldstandard3000: Ethan.

jladybugaboo: Do you have a plan? Which Methods of Flirtation are you going to use?

goldstandard3000: I don't know. Something quick.

jladybugaboo: Maybe giggling?

goldstandard3000: Something quicker. If I take more time, I'll have more time to mess it up.

jladybugaboo: Okay. So when are you going to do it?

goldstandard3000: Tomorrow.

News of Lydia and Ethan traveled fast, even though Jane was the only person that we told.

But Jane is pretty good at spreading information.

She's like a professional.

Roland found out pretty fast.

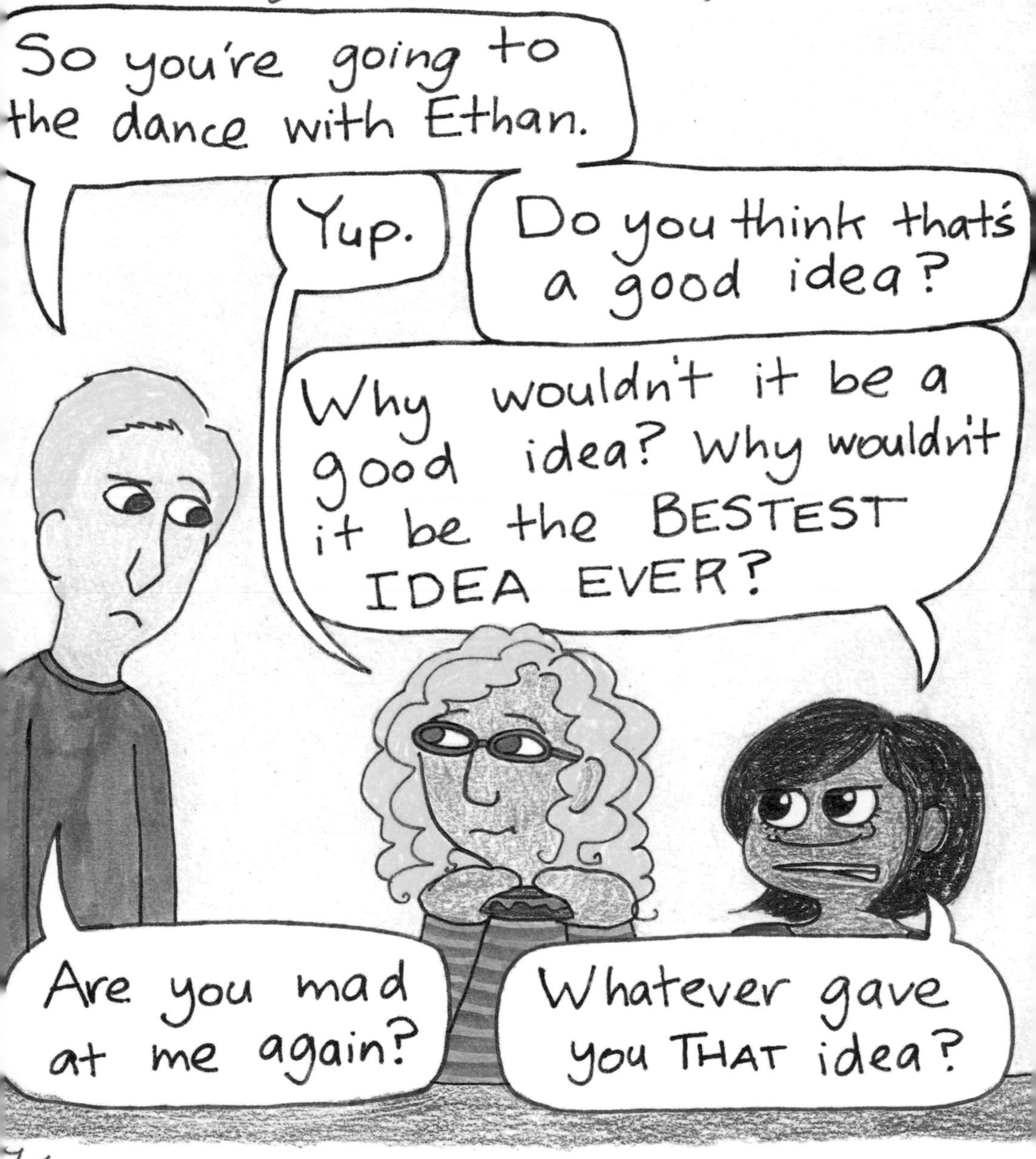

You can be kind of terrifying.

People are not happy about the whole Lydia/Ethan situation. But we expected that. It will probably settle down soon.

I really, really hope it settles down soon.

How are you holding up?

Okay, I guess. The only people who are talking to me are you, Jen, and Jane. Otherwise, everything is great.

It will pass.

Right. I would really like to get into my locker.

What do you need? I can ask for a bathroom pass and try to get it out of your locker.

Everything, I guess.

DEMERIT SLIP

Student's Name: Lydia Goldblatt

Date(s) 4.3   Time 2   Room ___

No. of Demerits: 1

Reason for Demerits: Walking wrong way down one-way hallway

Mrs. Sassaman
(Signature)

Again?
I'm carrying all of my books and my jacket and my travel mugs, and they still want me to walk all the way around the school? That's crazy.

Maybe you could bring less stuff to school.

If I do that, then they win. Okeedokey.

I've been scoping out my locker for the past few days, and it doesn't look like anyone is guarding it anymore, which is good, because my jacket is starting to smell like I've lined it with rotten eggs.

I think the coast is clear. I'm going to move my stuff back into my locker.

I do not trust your lockermate.

Maybe Chelsea shouldn't trust _me_. I can mess with her stuff just as easily as she can mess with mine.

But would you actually do it?

No, but she doesn't know that.

All the same, I think we should keep our journal in my locker for safekeeping.

Agreed.

Jamie Burke has been hanging out with Chelsea! This is so weird.
Why is it weird?
How can he be friends with her and me at the same time?
I guess the same way that you can be friends with Ethan and him at the same time.
I'm not friends with Ethan, we're just going to the dance together.
Everyone's just being friendly. Isn't that what you wanted?

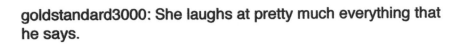

Do you think that Jamie is going to ask Chelsea to the dance? I'm beginning to think that no one besides you and maybe Gretchen want to go to the dance. Have you seen the notices?

<u>Attention Students. The Spring Dance will be held in the Gymnasium on Friday, May 20th, from 7-9pm. Formal wear is required. No jeans. There will be light refreshments.</u>

They couldn't even bother to use a full sheet of paper.

If no one is going to the dance, am I going to be stuck there alone with Ethan while Gretchen glares at us? We have to get more people to come. How?

DANCE PLANNING COMMITTEE

This is what the Dance Planning Committee looks like right now.

And this is what the Dance Planning Committee is going to look like.

The next committee meeting is tomorrow.

jladybugaboo: I am covered in glitter.

goldstandard3000: It's for a good cause.

jladybugaboo: But we've only made three posters. We need about twenty more.

goldstandard3000: We can do it!

jladybugaboo: I found glitter in my ear.

goldstandard3000: It's a small price to pay.

jladybugaboo: Yesterday I sneezed out some glitter.

goldstandard3000: Glamour mucus!

jladybugaboo: Stop trying to make glitter boogers seem cool. They're not. I can't make all these posters by myself.

goldstandard3000: Okay. I'll try to find some more people to help.

jladybugaboo: Thank you.

goldstandard3000: You're welcome, Sparkle Snot.

jladybugaboo: Please don't make Sparkle Snot a thing. It is not a thing.

You can't make all the posters but you can make all the pages in this book? Hush, priorities.

Getting people to help out hasn't been easy. It's not that people don't want to help...

It's that they don't want to help _me_

But you're so good at art.

Sorry Jules, but I just can't be seen with Lydia right now. Gretchen would kill me.

She wouldn't actually kill you for making some posters.

She'd ignore me. That's worse.

Making posters is a lot more fun with more people helping out.
Even Chris was getting into it, and he's only on the Dance Planning Committee because it was an alternative to after-school detention.

We should use more light green because, you know, the theme of the whole thing is supposed to be Spring, right?

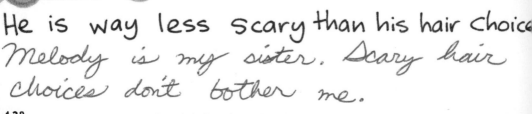

He is way less scary than his hair choice. Melody is my sister. Scary hair choices don't bother me.

Excellent! I think these are really going to help.
And maybe people will start liking you again.
PRING
ance
Friday, May
7 - 9 PM
That's the plan!
Or at least stop hating you.
That would also be nice.

The posters are actually making a difference. People are getting excited about the dance again, even if the Hamlin and Adams kids are still pretty unfriendly

Did you see Mrs. Foster today?

No. Why? Is there something wrong with the posters?

The posters are fine. But apparently being on the Dance Planning Committee means that we need to do more... planning.

For what?

We still need to plan for music, and refreshments, and decorations.

The next planning meeting is tomorrow after school. Don't be late.

jladybugaboo: We don't seriously have to go, do we?

goldstandard3000: I think we do. Chris has to go.

jladybugaboo: Chris is being forced to go by Principal Rao. We're not being forced by anyone.

goldstandard3000: I'm not so sure about that.

jladybugaboo: What do you mean?

goldstandard3000: You did not see the look in Suzy's eyes.

goldstandard3000: You never know, it might be fun. You helped plan my mom's wedding and that was fun, right?

WEDDING FLASHBACK

WE NEED MORE CREPE PAPER!!! WHERE IS THE CREPE PAPER???

I DON'T KNOW! WHY DO WE NEED CREPE PAPER???

I DON'T REMEMBER ANYMORE!!!

make it stop
oh please
make it stop

Less fun than you'd think.

The planning meeting was not fun.
It was a little fun at first.

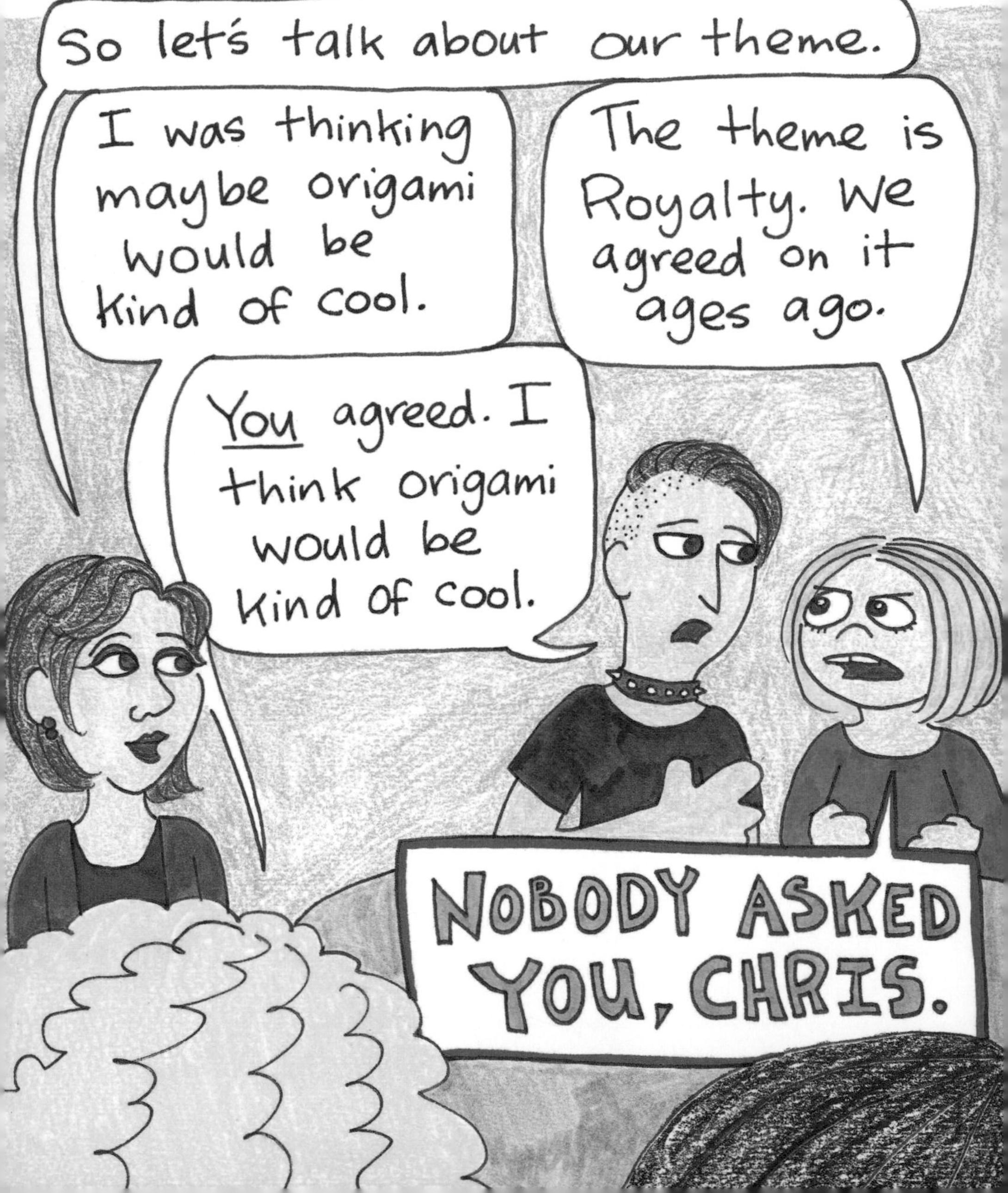

But then it got no fun at all.

goldstandard3000: Why do you think Stefan wants to be on the planning committee?

jladybugaboo: Because he's an evil trouble causer who is the cause of trouble.

goldstandard3000: I get that. But there has to be something else.

jladybugaboo: What do you mean?

goldstandard3000: I mean that he's got to have a specific plan to cause trouble.

jladybugaboo: Evil trouble causers don't make plans. They just cause trouble.

goldstandard3000: I feel like there's something more to it. There are much easier ways to cause trouble than joining the Spring Dance Planning Committee.

Hello committee. I really want to help out.

Then sit down, listen, and be prepared to work, because I don't have time to hold your hand while you figure out how to use glitter glue, m' kay?

I just...

SIT.

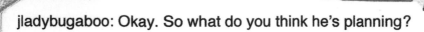

jladybugaboo: Okay. So what do you think he's planning?

goldstandard3000: I don't know.

Stefan's (possible) Nefarious Plan to RUIN the SPRING DANC[E]

1. Replace all of the good dance songs with weird Swiss experimental music.

Nefarious Plan # 2

Learn all the secrets and then plan an alternative, better dance for just the Adams kids.

Nefarious Plan #3

Plan to start a massive fight at the dance between the Hamlin and Adams kids

Bow tie? Check.
Hair gel? Check.
Violence in my heart? Check.
Cologne? Check.

You know, this scenario actually seems the most likely.

Yeah, I bet hot-air balloons are pretty expensive.

What are we going to do?

We have no real evidence that Stefan wants to cause trouble, but it seems really unlikely that he came to the planning meeting just to help plan. Although he did kind of try.

Somebody has to be in charge of making cupcakes. It's a lot of work, and they have to be perfect.

Wouldn't it be easier to just make a big cake and then cut a bunch of pieces?

MORE LISTENING, LESS TALKING, STEFAN. Fine, I'll just make the cupcakes myself.

If Stefan actually does anything to ruin the dance, Suzy is going to destroy him.

jladybugaboo: Do you have our journal?

goldstandard3000: No, you have it. Why, did you leave it at school?

jladybugaboo: No, I never leave it at school, I always take it home unless you take it home.

goldstandard3000: It's probably in your locker.

jladybugaboo: I really don't think it's in my locker. Are you sure it's not in your locker?

goldstandard3000: I'm pretty sure, but I'll check tomorrow.

jladybugaboo: I don't have it. I don't know where it is.

goldstandard3000: Stop panicking, it'll turn up tomorrow.

Did you find the journal?

No. It's not in my locker.

It's not in your locker?

NO IT ISN'T I DON'T HAVE IT.

Where did you last see it?

I don't know. Dance Planning Committee?

Okay. So we'll go to the student lounge after class. It's probably there. Maybe it's under a chair or something.

WHY WOULD IT BE UNDER A CHAIR OR SOMETHING??? WHY WOULD I LEAVE IT UNDER A CHAIR???

You have to calm down. We have to remain calm. We are going to figure this out. _Just_ _remain_ _calm_.

We are **NOT CALM.** It has been two days and there is no sign of our journal. We've checked **EVERYWHERE.**

Maybe we accidentally threw it out. Or we left it somewhere and the janitor threw it out.

At this point, that would probably be the best thing that could happen.

The journal was not thrown out.

DID YOU SEE IT? DID YOU SEE IT???

What? Did you find the journal?

I found a page from our journal. It was photocopied and hanging on the wall outside of the auditorium.

Oh my god. Did you tear it down?

OF COURSE I TORE IT DOWN.

Did anyone see it?

I don't know I don't know

What Page?

goldstandard3000: Did you hear from Jane yet?

THIS ONE

jladybugaboo: Not yet.

goldstandard3000: You know it's only a matter of time.

jladybugaboo: Oh, I'm already steeling myself for it.

Ugh, and I couldn't take it anymore, because you know how Chuck is always all blah blah and all I needed was a little blah blah blah, and he's just so blah bloooorp and seriously just unfair and blah nd Chuck just i or far be

Uh huh.

Sure.

goldstandard3000: She is going to be so annoying.

jladybugaboo: Well, we're just going to have to deal with it.

goldstandard3000: Brace yourself.

People saw it.
People definitely saw it.

It was awful.
Someone has our journal.
Someone awful.

jladybugaboo: I don't think I can go to school tomorrow.

goldstandard3000: I definitely don't want to go to school tomorrow.

jladybugaboo: I think I'm coming down with something.

goldstandard3000: I think I caught it from you.

jladybugaboo: Maybe it's a stomach bug.

goldstandard3000: Something is definitely going around.

jladybugaboo: Maybe we ate something weird.

goldstandard3000: We definitely ate something weird.

jladybugaboo: I think I should go to bed early.

goldstandard3000: Definitely tell your dads that you're going to bed early, they'll start to worry.

jladybugaboo: I definitely don't feel good.

goldstandard3000: I keep thinking about Jane. I don't feel good either.

You don't feel warm.

I might barf.

SICK DAY

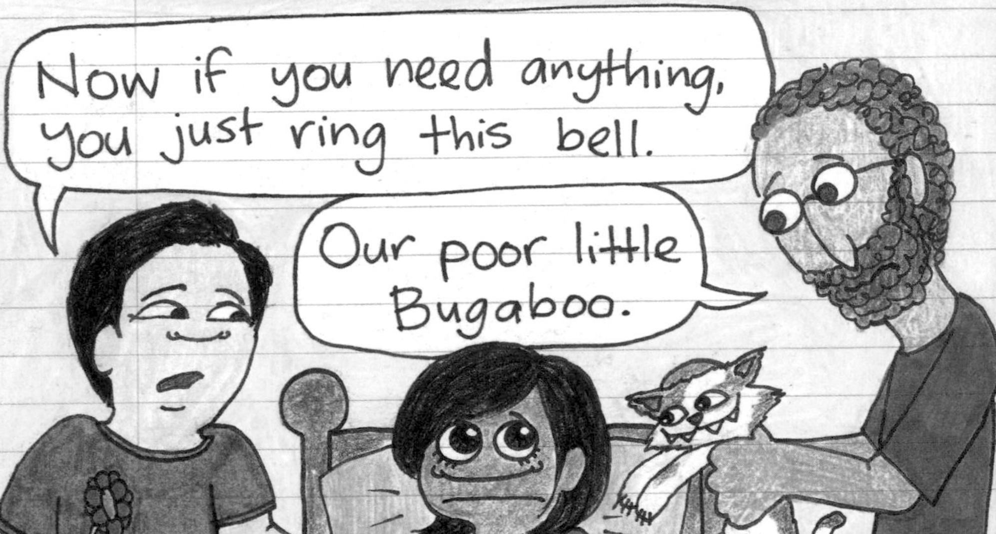

I definitely don't deserve this.

goldstandard3000: How was your day?

jladybugaboo: I feel terrible.

goldstandard3000: You're actually sick? I thought we were faking it to avoid Jane and school.

jladybugaboo: I feel terrible about Jane and school.

goldstandard3000: What are we going to do? We can't pretend to be sick forever. I don't think my mom actually really believed me this time.

jladybugaboo: We have to apologize to Jane.

goldstandard3000: We have to find out who photocopied our journal and put the pages up in the hallway.

jladybugaboo: Oh god oh god oh god. I think I'm getting sick again.

goldstandard3000: Me too.

jladybugaboo: Tomorrow is going to be awful.

goldstandard3000: It might not be so bad. Maybe nobody cares.

On second thought, it was no big deal?

And I love the way Julie drew my hair!

Boys are stupid.

I am Not untrustworthy or crazy. But I am getting really, really mad.

Have you seen any new pages?
I don't know. I feel sick again. Why
did we write all that stuff? What
else did we write?

Okay, breathe. You have to breathe.
Don't start crying in the middle
of Math. There's no crying in
Math.

We never should have kept that journal.
No. _Stop_. I love our journal.
When I was lonely in London,
writing in our journal kept me
from crying all the time. Maybe
we wrote some mean things, but
they were never meant to be seen
by other people because it was
a Private journal. It's Ours,
and someone horrible is ruining
it. We need to get it back.

WHAT I FOUND IN MY LOCKER

Hey Julie,

Isn't it cool to see your work all over the school? There's more where that came from!

jladybugaboo: What are we going to do?

goldstandard3000: We have to get our journal back.

jladybugaboo: How??? We don't even know who took it!

goldstandard3000: Someone is putting up those posters. We just have to catch them in the act.

jladybugaboo: How????

goldstandard3000: Stakeout.

THE PLAN

Get to school early and hide on opposite ends of the school. Catch the thief in the act of putting up the copied pages.

We will need:

1. Our cell phones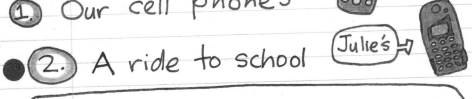

2. A ride to school

Say, Declan, are your parents letting you drive the car again?

THE SUSPECTS

1. Chelsea

Motive: She hates us, is mean, and has access to everything in Lydia's locker.

2. Stefan

Motive: Is a great big jerk, might have taken the book during the planning meeting.

3. The Butler

Motive: The butler needs no motive but should always be a suspect.

jladybugaboo: Declan is definitely going to bring us tomorrow?

goldstandard3000: Yep. I told him and Melody that we needed to get to school early to hang more dance signs.

jladybugaboo: Okay. So do we have a plan?

goldstandard3000: I thought the plan was to find the thief and get our book back.

jladybugaboo: How would we get the book back?

goldstandard3000: We would take it back?

jladybugaboo: But how?

goldstandard3000: I don't know. With our hands?

jladybugaboo: Are we going to beat the person up?

goldstandard3000: No! Probably not.

jladybugaboo: PROBABLY not?

goldstandard3000: Look, if we have to, I'll pin the culprit while you search their bag. We'll try not to cause injury. Are you okay with that?

Okay.

At first the stakeout was kind of exciting.

Goldbladder 1, this is Ladybug 1. Goldbladder 1, come in. Over.

Then it got kind of boring.

They should paint these hallways a more interesting color. This gray purple is killing me.

And then I saw HIM.

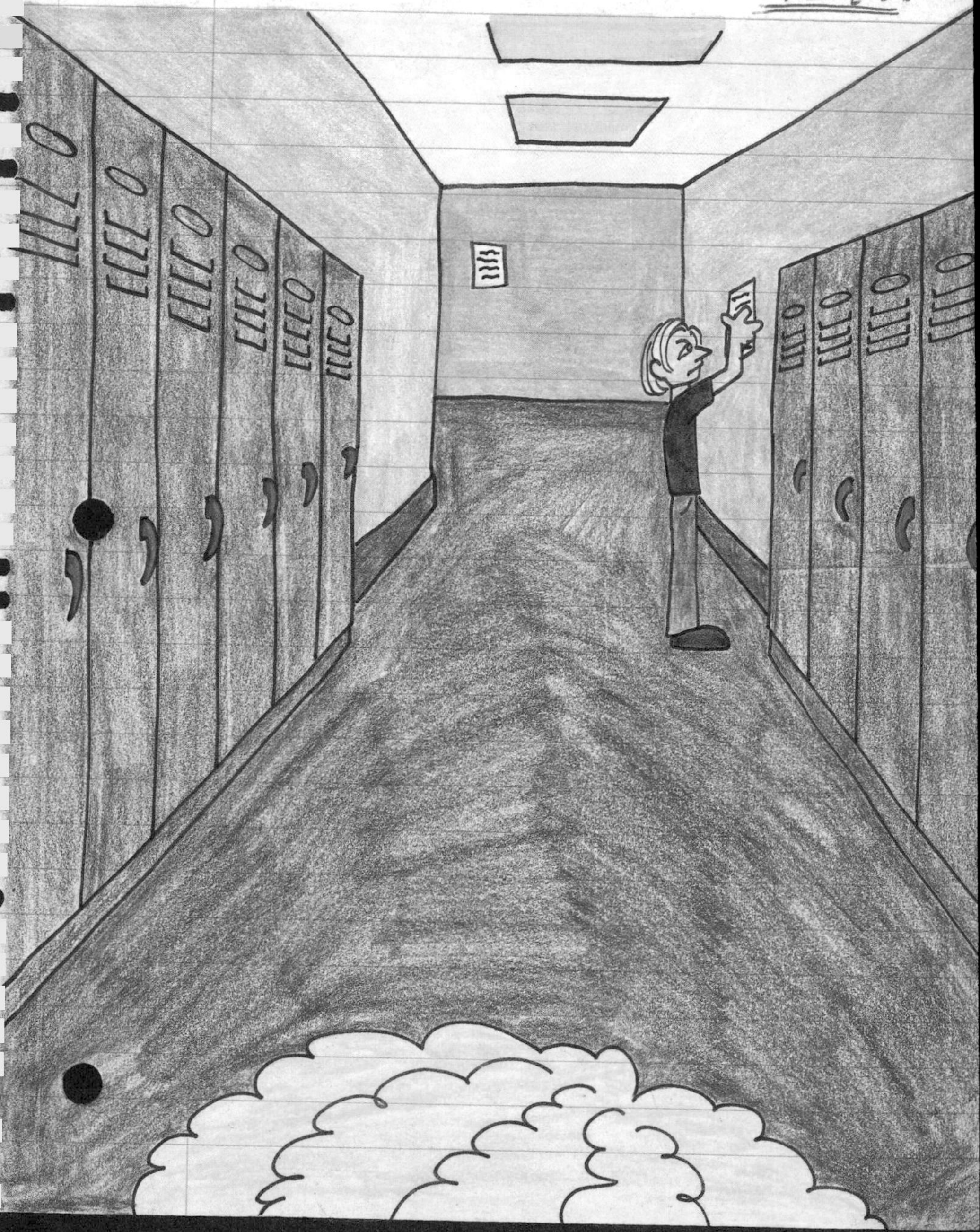

What Actually Happened
HARBALAR BAJOORNUL MIIIINE BA BLAAAARRRR!!!
It was slightly less cool.
You were terrifying.
Well, thats' something.

Stefan almost got away.
Almost.
YOU GIVE ME BACK MY JOURNAL, YOU AWFUL SWISS! WHERE IS IT???

I can't believe I did that. I can't believe it took me, Mrs. Sassaman, and a school security guard to pry you off of him.

I can't believe we have detention. I can believe that. I am an unrepentant violator of the one-way hallway rule and you are a rabid howler monkey.

Our parents are going to kill us. A lot.

She did WHAT???

Detention Essay
by Julie Graham-Chang

I am very, very sorry that I attacked another student. I was really angry at the other student, and he had taken something important from me, but I know now that doesn't justify my violent actions. While I would like very much for Stefan to give me back my thing, he swears that he doesn't have it and I have to accept that. I am very sorry and I will not beat Stefan up again, even though he is clearly a big liar.

Detention Essay
by Lydia Goldblatt

No more going the wrong way down the one-way hallway for me. The end.

Detention was the boringest.

It would have been worth it if we had just gotten our journal back. It was all for nothing.

Not nothing. I think Stefan is probably too scared of you to put up any new pages.

But he still has our journal.

But then...

It's back! Our journal is back! I found it in my locker!

What? How? WHAT???

It was just in my locker.

How did it get there?

I don't know and I don't care.

jladybugaboo: I'm definitely never bringing the book to school again, but I'm starting to wonder if it's even good to keep a book like this.

goldstandard3000: But I like being able to record all our adventures and thoughts. It helps me figure stuff out.

jladybugaboo: Sure, but now Jane hates us and everyone in the school thinks we talk about them all the time.

goldstandard3000: But everyone talks about everyone else all the time. We were just unlucky enough to get caught.

jladybugaboo: We weren't "caught," we were EXPOSED. By writing everything out we left ourselves really vulnerable.

goldstandard3000: But no one knew what we were doing!

jladybugaboo: Stefan did! Maybe we weren't as sneaky as we thought we were.

This is how sneaky we thought we were:

This is how sneaky we actually are:

So everyone knows what we've been up to, and now that Stefan photocopied our pages and put them up everywhere, everyone knows EXACTLY what we've been up to.

And nobody likes it.

There's no way we're going to the dance.

Things We Can Do Instead of Going to the SPRING DANCE

1. Cry.

2. Watch teevee and cry.

3. Have our own dance party.

I think we have to go to the dance.

What are you talking about?

We had a whole awesome crying plan.

Suzy found me.

Oh no.

You and Lydia are on the planning committee. You have responsibilities. YOU WILL BE THERE. And you're coming to the next committee meeting.

She's just so scary. I know!

At least Roland is happy about going to the dance.

Last Planning Committee Meeting

So, that didn't go well.
No, it did not.

We have a **PROBLEM**.

It seems that some students from Adams would like to have a separate dance, and some students from Hamlin are supporting this plan.

This is **BAD**, people. **BAD**.

We will not be holding two separate dances, but this is concerning.

nobuddy
pay
attention
to me

I'm hardly
even here

goldstandard3000: We have to come up with some sort of plan to get us through the dance.

jladybugaboo: I was thinking that maybe we find a good place to hide and curl up into little balls while our classmates tear each other limb from limb.

goldstandard3000: That is a plan, but maybe we should come up with something a little less wussy.

jladybugaboo: Fine. We don't have to curl up into little balls. We can just hide in the girls' bathroom all night.

goldstandard3000: I don't think our date would appreciate that so much.

jladybugaboo: Hang on, the dads are calling me down for a talk. See you tomorrow.

CATASTROPHE!

Great news! I just got off the phone with Mrs. Foster, and you are looking at a brand-new Spring Dance chaperone!
You are kidding me.
Isn't it great? I gave her Lydia's phone number so that Eric or Elaine could also be chaperones.
This is the worst joke ever.
We are going to have SO MUCH FUN!

What's worse than going to a social event where everyone hates everyone else and it's guaranteed that terrible, terrible things will happen?

HAVING YOUR PARENTS THERE.

This is brilliant! James wants us to wear some sort of special tie or pin or something so everyone knows that you and Julie are our kids.

Oh, I know I'm not your real da, but I can still be proud of you, yeah?

What are we going to do?

My curling up into a little ball plan is looking better and better, isn't it?

What do you think Papa Dad meant by "some sort of special tie or pin or something"?

Whatever it is, it can't be good.

Official Chaperone Contract

You, ___James Graham___, as Official Chaperone of the Hamlin Junior High Spring Dance, do solemnly swear to follow these simple rules:

1. There will be no interaction with students or teachers unless absolutely necessary. This includes:
   a. Pointing out that you are related to anyone else at the dance
   b. Singing along with dance songs
   c. Teaching students really, really, really old dance moves

2. You will dress appropriately:
   a. Shirt, tie
   b. No homemade pins
   c. NO NOVELTY TEE SHIRTS
   d. No weird hats

   No pants?

   You have to wear pants!!!

3. There will be no acknowledgment of any family members who are present (except for when dropping them off and driving them home).

4. NO TAKING PICTURES WITH YOUR CELL PHONE.

5. NO SHOWING ANYONE ELSE PICTURES THAT YOU'VE TAKEN WITH YOUR CELL PHONE.

Thank you for your compliance.

X _James Graham_

The only thing left to do is decorate.

This doesn't look good.
But you have to admit, Chris is
kind of a genius with crepe paper.
He really does have a gift.

NIGHT of the SPRING DANCE
6:15 PM
We all met up at Roland's house to take photos.
So Jen... What are you wearing?
It's formal wear. Do you like it?
You look very nice!
Thanks!
I'm not crying!

7:00 PM

When we got to the gym, the Adams kids were dancing because it was their DJ's turn. The Hamlin kids were refusing to dance.

I thought everyone would be staring at us, but everyone was too busy glaring at the Adams kids.

So that went on for a while.

And then it got kind of... Fun!

GO JAMIE! GO JAMIE! GO JAMIE! GO JAMIE!

GO MASON! GO MASON! GO MASON! GO MASON!

I don't know who that Mason guy was, but he could really dance.

And thus began

Marisol, I didn't know you were such an amazing dancer!
Could you maybe show me some moves? I really don't know what I'm doing.
Umm, thanks.
Julie, I have to tell you something.

larisol was the one who stole our book.

I thought it would make Stefan like me.

Do you like him???

No! I just wanted him to stop making fun of me. But I stole the book back after he put up those photocopies. I'm so sorry.

I didn't know what to say to her. I felt sorry for her, but I was so mad. *Me too.*

The rest of the dance was actually fun.
Dance with me, my love!
Wait. Since when am I your "love"?
Since always. I've asked you out fifty-seven times.
HAVING A PICNIC ON THE MOON IS NOT A SERIOUS DATE!
Says who?
Oh dear god.
Fine, let's dance.

All of a sudden everyone was dancing to our music! "Music" is one word for it.

We sound awesome! I totally love you guys!

I thought you were mad at...

We love you, too!

Just go with it.

Is it just me or is everything way more complicated than it was in elementary school? It's not just you.

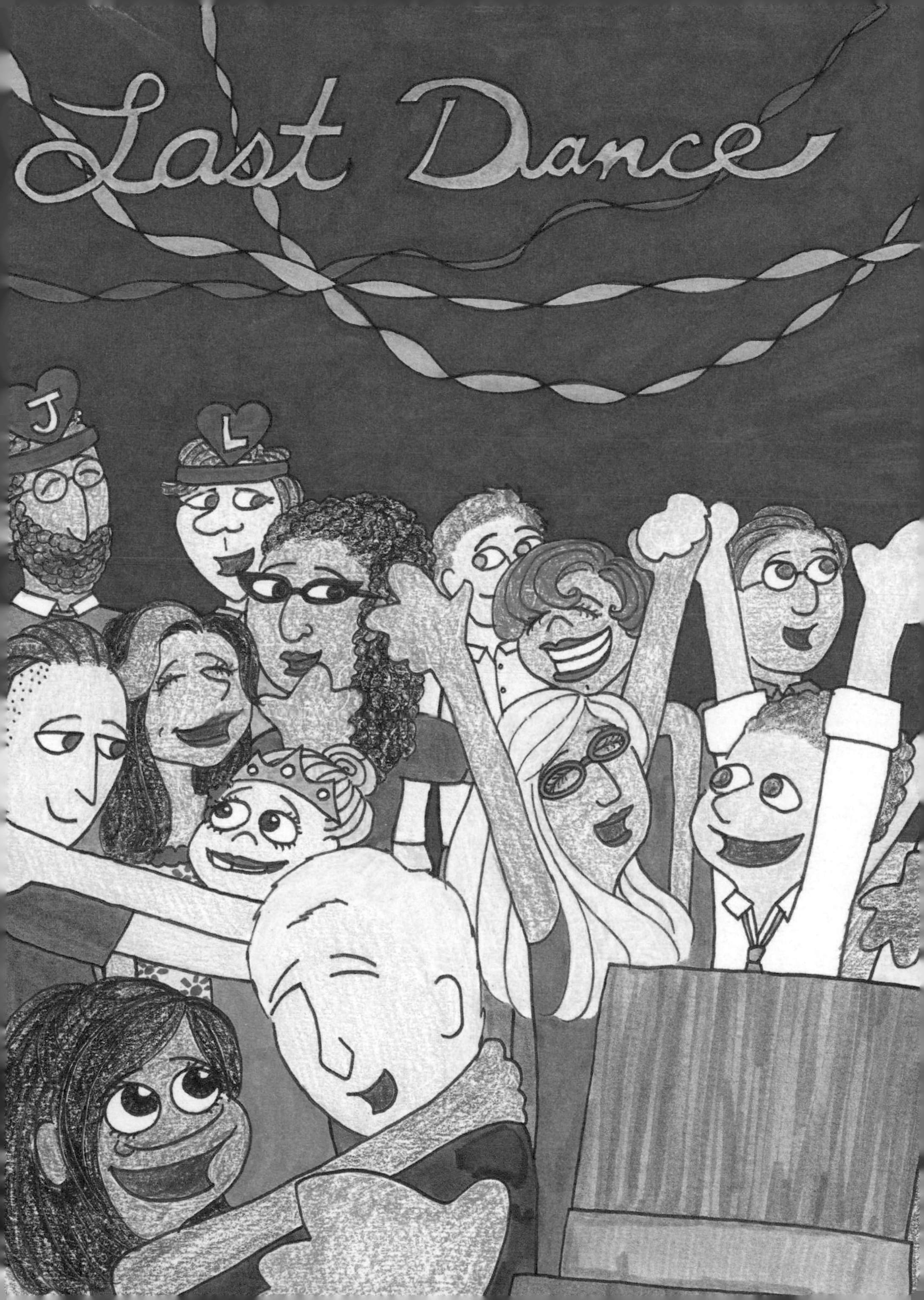
Last Dance
J
L

The lake was full of kids from school, and both Hamlin and Adams kids were having a great time.

So our plan to make everyone get along worked.

I don't know how much of that was actually us.

Hush. We're geniuses.

I still kind of don't get why everyone isn't still mad at us.
are you still mad at Marisol?
I don't know. Not really.
It's hard to be mad when it's such a nice day out.
Staying mad all the time seems like too much work.
Doesn't seem worth it.
Exactly.

I can't believe 7th grade is almost over.
We're so much wiser than when we started.
Just one more year and then high school. Crazy.
So we've got just one more year o prepare ourselves! High school s really different— we should start observing the high school kids right now...

HIGH SCHOOL KIDS
Initial Observations

1. They're bigger than us.

2. Some of the boys have facial hair.

You've got a little something on your chin.

It's a goatee.

Well, whaddaya know!

Otherwise, they're pretty much the same as us.

Confused, freaked out, excited, and full of hope?

That sounds about right.

Then we're ready!

Acknowledgments

Great oceans of my gratitude are due to the wonderful team at Amulet Books: Susan Van Metre, Jen Graham, Jessie Gang, Chris Blank, Chad Beckerman, Laura Mihalick, Morgan Dubin, and the most very splendid Jason Wells. I cannot give enough thanks to Maggie Lehrman, my editor and friend, who is as enthusiastic about Lydia and Julie today as she was when we started this journey six years ago.

Forever thanks go to the inexhaustible Dan Lazar, who claims to take vacations in the work emails he sends me while on vacation, as well as Torie Doherty-Munro and all the wonderful people at Writers House. Thanks as well to Deborah Gardner, my old friend who at my request cheerfully sends blank postcards from foreign climes with nary a question as to why, and to all my family and friends who believed in me when doing so seemed unbelievable.

And of course thanks to my wonderful and supportive husband, Mark, and our very funny daughter, Anya.

About the Author

Amy Ignatow is the author and illustrator of The Popularity Papers series. She is a graduate of Moore College of Art and Design, and once made a really pretty lump during a glassblowing class. Amy lives in Philadelphia with her husband, Mark, their daughter, Anya, and their cat, Mathilda, who might possibly mean well. Maybe. But probably not.

To all the Lydias and Julies and Rolands and Melodys
and Janes and Papa Dads and everyone else who has ever
read and related to my books
—Ig

Artist's Note: The materials used to create the book
are ink, colored pencil, colored marker, and digital.

PUBLISHER'S NOTE: This is a work of fiction. Names, characters, places, and incidents are either the
product of the author's imagination or are used fictitiously, and any resemblance to actual persons,
living or dead, business establishments, events, or locales is entirely coincidental.

Library of Congress Control Number: 2014936061

ISBN for this edition: 978-1-4197-1357-6

Text and illustrations copyright © 2014 Amy Ignatow
Book design by Amy Ignatow and Jessie Gang

Printed and bound in China
10 9 8 7 6 5 4 3 2 1

Amulet Books are available at special discounts when purchased in quantity for premiums and
promotions as well as fundraising or educational use. Special editions can also be created to
specification. For details, contact specialsales@abramsbooks.com or the address below.

ABRAMS
THE ART OF BOOKS SINCE 1949
115 West 18th Street
New York, NY 10011
www.abramsbooks.com